Ellie ☆ Sandall

EVERYBUNNY
ance!

Nobody is watching.
Now's the perfect chance.

Ready bunny,

steady bunny,

EVERYBUNNY

DANCE!

And **clap** your paws,

and **twist** and **twirl**,

and **shake** your tail,

and **wiggle** and **whirl**.

And **bang** a drum,

and **play** the flute,

and blow a horn,

a-tooty-toot!

Fa-la-la-la, tra-la-la-lee,

doo-dooby-doo, fiddle-de...

FOX!

EVERYBUNNY

RUN!

Stay very still,
don't make a sound,
hold your breath
or you'll be found.

Everybunny
watch...

a dainty waltz,

a pirouette,

a somersault,

a clarinet,

a graceful bow,

a quiet sigh,

a lonely fox,

a tearful eye.

EVERYBUNNY CLAP!

And gather round,
and cheer and sing,
and call 'Bravo',
and all join in!

And run and jump,
and dance and play,

all together,

every day.

for Brian

HODDER CHILDREN'S BOOKS

First published in Great Britain in 2016 by Hodder and Stoughton

Text and illustrations copyright © Ellie Sandall 2016

The moral rights of the author and illustrator have been asserted.

A CIP catalogue record of this book
is available from the British Library.

HB ISBN: 978 1 444 91986 8
PB ISBN: 978 1 444 91987 5

10 9 8 7 6 5 4 3 2 1

Printed and bound in China

Hodder Children's Books
An imprint of
Hachette Children's Group
Part of Hodder and Stoughton
Carmelite House
50 Victoria Embankment
London EC4Y 0DZ

An Hachette UK Company
www.hachette.co.uk

www.hachettechildrens.co.uk